# THE LONG AND THE SHORT OF IT

## A TALE ABOUT HAIR

# THE LONG AND THE SHORT OF IT

## A TALE ABOUT HAIR

By Barbara Meyers & Lydia Criss Mays
Illustrated by Shennen Bersani

American Cancer Society®

Published by the American Cancer Society
Health Promotions
250 Williams Street NW
Atlanta, GA 30303-1002

Manufactured by Transcontinental Interglobe
Manufactured in Beauceville, QC, Canada
Job #52290

Printed in Canada

5 4 3 2 1    11 12 13 14 15

Library of Congress Cataloging-in-Publication Data
Meyers, Barbara.
  The long and the short of it : a tale about hair / by Barbara Meyers and Lydia Criss Mays.
     p. cm.
  ISBN-13: 978-1-60443-017-2 (hardcover : alk. paper)
  ISBN-10: 1-60443-017-6 (hardcover : alk. paper)
  1. Cancer in children—Juvenile literature. 2. Baldness—Juvenile literature. 3. Cancer—Chemotherapy—Side effects—Juvenile literature. I. Mays, Lydia Criss. II. Title.
  RC281.C4M49 2010
  616.99'4061—dc22
                          2010043999

**AMERICAN CANCER SOCIETY**
Managing Director, Content: Chuck Westbrook
Director, Cancer Information: Terri Ades, DNP, FNP-BC, AOCN
Director, Book Publishing: Len Boswell
Managing Editor, Books: Rebecca Teaff, MA
Editor, Books: Jill Russell
Book Publishing Coordinator: Vanika Jordan, MSPub
Editorial Assistant, Books: Amy Rovere

Book Design by Jill Ronsley, Sun Editing & Book Design, www.suneditwrite.com

For more information about cancer, contact your American Cancer Society at
**800-227-2345** or **cancer.org**.

Quantity discounts on bulk purchases of this book are available. Book excerpts can also be created to fit specific needs. For information, please contact the American Cancer Society, Health Promotions Publishing, 250 Williams Street NW, Atlanta, GA 30303-1002, or send an e-mail to **trade.sales@cancer.org**.

***From Barbara and Lydia***

This story was inspired by two little girls, Isabel and Emma.
This book is dedicated to our families,
as well as to all families whose lives have been affected by cancer.


***From Shennen***

To my daughters, Karlene and Kerrin,
for generously donating their hair—a couple of times—to Locks of Love.

I'm Isabel. My eyes are the color of the sea and my hair is the color of caramel candy. People tell me my hair is straight as bamboo. When I was five, I lived in Illinois with my mother, father, and big brother, Charlie. Mom said I was ready to use a real knife when we cooked in the kitchen. Dad helped me try out a two-wheeler with training wheels, and Charlie practiced chess with me because I was old enough to join the chess team.

I'm Emma. I have big, round brown eyes. When I was five I had straight blond hair and when I smiled you could see the hole in my mouth where I lost my first tooth. I lived in Georgia with my mom, my dad, my brother, Calvin, and my sister, Audrey. Mom told me I was big enough to keep an eye on Baby Audrey while she worked in the garden. Dad even let me go to work with him sometimes, and Calvin taught me how to rock climb because I was strong enough.

When I started kindergarten, I felt really grown up. I decided it was time to grow my hair long, just like my twelve-year-old cousins Gina and Alexa. They had long, shiny hair that went down their backs and swayed when they danced. I always wished my hair swayed just like theirs. I didn't know it yet, but I was also old enough to have patience.

## The thing about growing out your hair is it takes a long, long time!

I was so excited about going to kindergarten. I *loved* when Ms. Goff taught us math. It was my favorite time of the day. Just after I started school, I got sick. When I used to get sick, my mom would give me medicine and I'd get better right away. But this time, I didn't feel better. The doctor told my family I had cancer. To get better I would have to take a special medicine every day. The medicine made my hair fall out. It got really thin and stringy, like dental floss. I loved my hair, and I really didn't want my hair to go away. But Dad told me being bald is fun. He doesn't have hair either, but not because he's sick. There are lots of reasons people don't have hair.

## The thing about losing your hair is that it can make you feel sad.

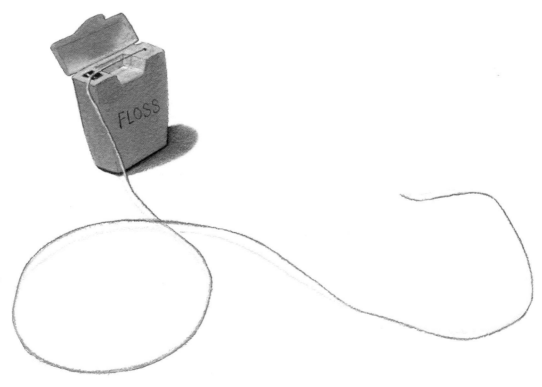

Mom said I could grow my hair long, but I would have to take care of it and brush it every day and every night. So I shampooed and conditioned my hair, combed out the knots, and even used a special spray called a detangler. My hair looked like Rapunzel's, and I used barrettes, bows, and headbands. When Grandma came to town, we went shopping for beautiful ribbons. When I played soccer, my mom put my hair in a ponytail or French braid so I could see the ball and score a goal.

## The thing about having long hair is that it can be fun, but taking care of it can be a lot of work.

As I kept taking the medicine, I lost more and more hair. At night it would fall out on my pillow. I didn't have as much energy for rock climbing or playing with my friends, but I still loved helping Mom make brownies and cookies. The doctors said I was getting better because of the medicine, so I had to keep taking it. My hair kept falling out. I didn't want it to keep happening every night, so I asked my mom if we could shave it off. We went to the hair salon, and I held the clippers to cut my own hair. I wanted to see what I looked like with only a Mohawk. It was funny, but it wasn't really the hairstyle for me.

## The thing about losing your hair is you have to have a sense of humor.

My best friend had long hair like me. We loved to dress up as princesses and fix our hair in lots of different ways. One day she came to school with short hair. I didn't even recognize her! She told me she had given her hair away. Huh? It had taken me months and months to grow out my hair. I would never want to give it away! But then she told me what happened to her hair after she cut it off. She told me that some kids get very sick, and they lose their hair. If you grow your hair really long, you can donate it to a group that makes wigs for children who have lost their hair. That got me thinking about whether someone could use my hair. I wondered if my hair was long enough to give away. I liked the idea of doing nice stuff for someone else.

## The thing about growing out your hair is that some people do it just to give it to others.

After I lost my hair, I did not like going to school. Mom and Dad asked why, and I told them my embarrassing story. Someone at school asked me if I was a boy or a girl because I didn't have any hair. She said, "You're wearing pink like a girl, but you look like a boy." That made me sad, but I didn't cry. I told her I was a girl. I didn't want people to know how upset I was, but I wanted my hair back! I was the same Emma, even though I looked really different. Mom said she was proud of me because I told the girl without getting upset. Still, it was a sad day for me.

### The thing about losing your hair is it can make you feel embarrassed.

I told my mom about my friend's haircut and why she gave her hair away. I kept thinking about the children who had lost their hair. I was worried. Could I get sick with something that would make my beautiful hair go away? Could I catch cancer and lose *my* hair? I wouldn't be able to go get beautiful ribbons with Grandma or have fancy hairdos. Mom said that people don't catch cancer. She said, "We know you are healthy. We have taken you for checkups. If you get sick, Dr. Sanchez will tell us how to help you get better."

## The thing about your hair is it can be scary to think about not having any.

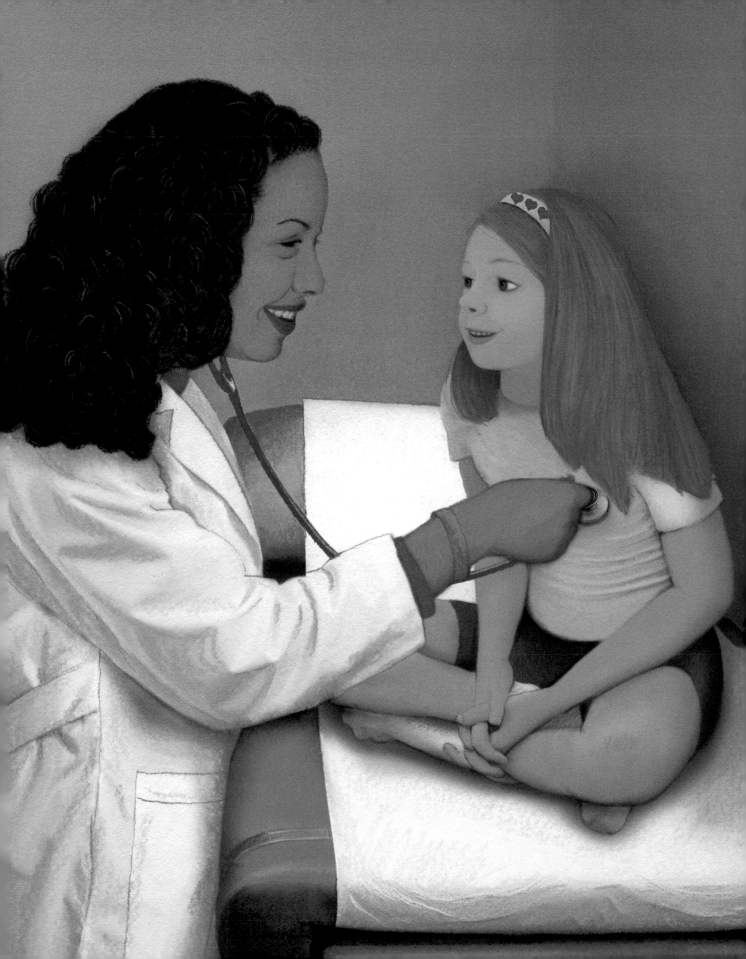

I felt better and better every day. I was able to go to Camp Sunshine for a week over the summer. It's an awesome place for kids like me who have cancer. We swam, played games, and slept in tents just like other kids. But I still felt embarrassed. When I looked at myself in the mirror, I felt weird. Mom and Dad tried all sorts of things to make me feel better about my bald head. Mom bought me lots of colorful bandanas, and we went to the store and picked out fun, pretty hats. Even though the bandanas and hats covered my head, people still looked at me funny.

## The thing about losing your hair is you have to be creative.

Even though I'd worked so hard to grow my hair long, I got this idea that maybe someone else needed it more than I did. I asked my mom to measure my hair to see if it was long enough to give away. It had to be ten inches long before I could donate it. My ponytail was only eight inches long. I had two inches to go.

We kept on measuring. My hair grew and grew, and sometimes it got so tangled that my mom wanted to cut it. But donating it was too important. I had to wait until it was just the right length.

## The thing about deciding to give your hair to someone is that you have to go for it and not give up.

DETANGLER

Then, something wonderful happened! I got a wig made out of real hair. It reminded me of my own hair. Now I felt like my old self again. The wig came from children and adults who grew out their hair and donated it. Even though I didn't know who gave their hair, I could tell they cared about people like me. My doctors said the medicine was working, but I wasn't well yet. This meant I had to keep taking the medicine, and my own hair couldn't start growing back yet. Good thing I had my wig!

**The thing about having hair, even if it wasn't really from my own head, was that it made me feel SO much better!**

My hair finally, finally, finally measured ten inches! Woohoo! I was so excited. It was the right length to cut. We went to the hair salon and I waited my turn. When they called out "Isabel," I went with my mom and sat in the chair. The haircut lady said it was a tricky cut because she had to cut so close to my head. I was a little afraid that the haircut might hurt, but it didn't. I felt like a new me with my new short hair!

## The thing about getting your hair cut is that it doesn't hurt.

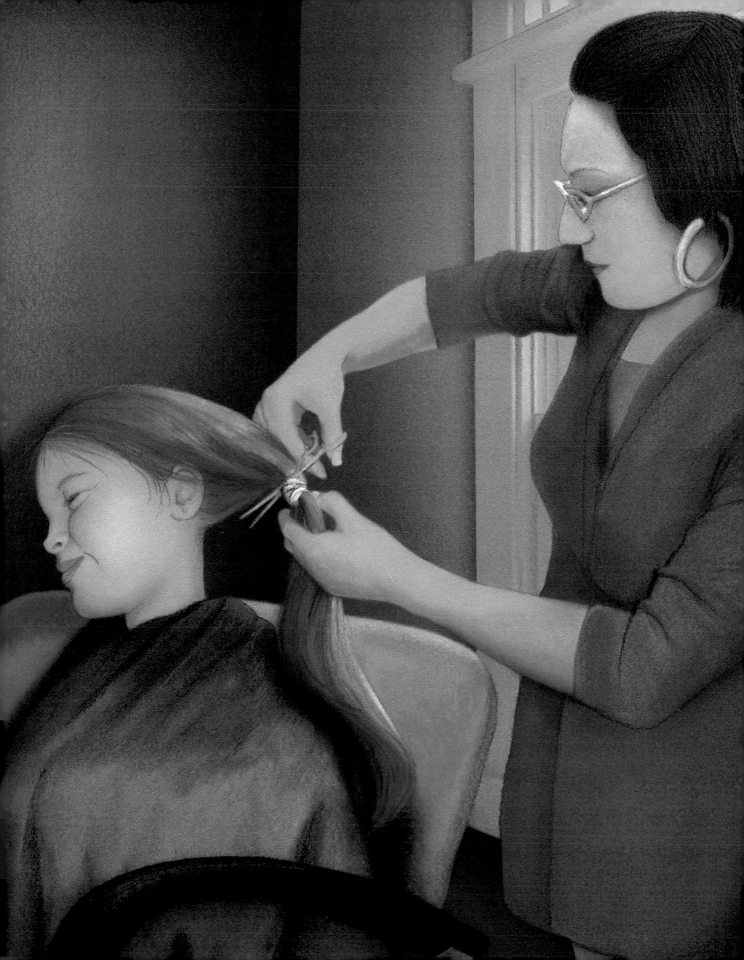

I loved having hair, but the wig was sort of itchy. So my friends made this thing called a ponytail pack for me from their own hair. They sewed the hair onto a ponytail holder and then onto a cap. It was cool! Now I could wear my wig or my ponytail pack. I started to feel well enough to do things with my family. We went out to dinner at my favorite restaurant and visited the park in my neighborhood. No one asked me whether I was a boy or a girl. They knew!

## The thing about having a wig or ponytail pack is that I was happy and felt like me again.

I kinda liked my short hair. In the summer, it was cooler and easier to wash and brush. I had more time to play with my dolls, ride my two-wheeler, and read books all by myself.

Sometimes, I missed my long hair, but I knew I could grow it long again. I don't know who got my hair after I cut it, but that's okay. If someone loves my hair as much as I did, it was worth it.

## The thing about giving away your hair is that it makes you feel good.

My family finally got good news! The doctors said my cancer was gone. I could stop taking the medicine that made my hair fall out. My hair grew back brown and curly. I loved it! My hair used to be blond and straight, like everyone else's in my family. But that's okay; my different hair made me feel pretty cool.

I decided to grow my new hair long so that I could donate it to others who had lost their hair just like I did.

**The thing about having your own hair again is that now you have something to grow and give to others, too. And now you're well.**

# Reading and Discussion Guide for Adults

This book was designed to teach children about hair loss and the act of giving; to recognize and express feelings of fear, frustration, courage, and patience; to encourage open communication between children and adults; and to help adults examine common misconceptions children may have about cancer and hair loss. As we described the parallel stories of Isabel and Emma, we intentionally embedded critical concepts on each page of *The Long and the Short of It: A Tale About Hair*. The concepts and related page numbers are listed below:

| *Concept* | *Page* |
| --- | --- |
| Ambivalence | 13, 30 |
| Cancer | 9, 13, 14, 17, 18, 21, 25, 29, 33 |
| Courage | 9, 13, 26 |
| Creativity | 13, 21, 29 |
| Fear | 9, 13, 18, 26 |
| Friendship | 14, 21, 29 |
| Frustration | 9, 13, 17, 21 |
| Generosity | 14, 22, 25, 26, 29, 30, 33 |
| Goal setting | 10, 22 |
| Patience | 6, 10, 22, 25, 26 |
| Persistence | 10, 22 |
| Pride | 26, 29, 30, 33 |
| Responsibility | 10, 14, 22, 33 |
| Sadness | 9, 17, 21 |
| Solving problems | 9, 13, 14, 21, 25, 29 |
| Uniqueness | 2, 5, 9, 17, 21, 33 |
| Wellness | 9, 13, 18, 25, 29, 33 |

# Critical Thinking Activities for Children

1. Draw a picture of yourself with hair, with a wig, and bald. Discuss feelings associated with each look.

2. Try on a wig and look in the mirror. How do you look? How does it feel?

3. Think about something you have that is very special. Talk about it and why it is important. Would you give it away? Why?

4. Emma felt sad when her school friends teased her because she looked different from them. Have you ever been teased? Felt embarrassed? What did you do?

5. Isabel had to wait a very long time for her hair to grow. She had to be patient. Is there something you had to wait for? Was it worth the wait? Why?

6. Would you like to give your hair to someone who needs it? Check out these Web sites*:

   a) *Childhood Leukemia Foundation:* http://www.clf4kids.com
   b) *Children with Hair Loss:* http://childrenwithhairloss.us
   c) *Locks of Love:* http://www.locksoflove.org
   d) *Pantene Beautiful Lengths:* http://www.beautifullengths.com/en_US
   e) *Wigs 4 Kids:* http://www.wigs4kids.org
   f) *Wigs for Kids:* http://www.wigsforkids.org

7. Would you like to help others? Who needs your help? Brainstorm ideas and come up with ways to help others.

* Inclusion on this list does not imply endorsement by the American Cancer Society.

# About the Girls

**Isabel** is nine years old and in fourth grade. She loves helping in the garden and going on bike rides and to the movies with her family. Some of her favorite things are the color aqua, fawns, the television show *iCarly*, books by Rick Riordan, and macaroni and cheese. After donating her hair, she decided to keep it short for a while. But now her hair is growing back and is a little past her shoulders. She is planning a second donation when her hair is long enough.

**Emma** is thirteen years old and in the eighth grade. She loves to hang out with her friends and go to the movies, but Emma's favorite thing is her week at Camp Sunshine. At Camp Sunshine, she connects with others who have battled cancer and enjoys an amazing variety of activities, including spa night and horseback riding. One summer, she even got to do circus acts, instructed by professional circus performers! Emma had the privilege of donating her post-chemotherapy hair to Locks of Love.

# About the Authors

**Barbara Meyers, EdD,** is Isabel's grandmother. She is chair of the Department of Early Childhood Education at Georgia State University and has been an educator for more than forty years. She loves to read, beach comb, and cook, especially with Isabel, Isabel's brother, Charlie, and their cousins Jakey and Hailey. She lives in Atlanta, Georgia, with her husband, Joel.

**Lydia Criss Mays, PhD,** is a friend of Emma's. She was an elementary school teacher in Tennessee and Georgia and recently earned her doctoral degree in early childhood education from Georgia State University, where she now teaches. She loves spending time with her family, biking, and hiking. Like Emma and Isabel, she has donated her hair—four times! She lives in Atlanta, Georgia, with her husband, Andrew, and her two dogs, Lilly and Buddy.

# About the Illustrator

**Shennen Bersani,** award-winning children's book illustrator, has had two million copies of her illustrated books cherished and read by families throughout the world. A cancer survivor, Shennen drew inspiration from her own life to illustrate two previous books for the American Cancer Society, *Let My Colors Out* and *Nana, What's Cancer?* Shennen's beautiful illustrations also can be found in a variety of other well-known children's books, including *Astro: The Stellar Sea Lion; Ocean Counting: Odd Numbers; Snakes: Long, Longer, Longest;* and *My Sister, Alicia May.* Shennen lives with her family near Boston, Massachusetts.

# Other Books for Children from the American Cancer Society

Available everywhere books are sold and online at
**cancer.org/bookstore**

*Because … Someone I Love Has Cancer*
*Get Better! Communication Cards for Kids & Adults*
*Healthy Me: A Read-Along Coloring & Activity Book*
*Kids' First Cookbook: Delicious-Nutritious Treats to Make Yourself!*
*Let My Colors Out*
*Mom and the Polka-Dot Boo-Boo*
*Nana, What's Cancer?*
*No Thanks, but I'd Love to Dance: Choosing to Live Smoke Free*
*Our Dad Is Getting Better*
*Our Mom Has Cancer (available in hard cover and paperback)*
*Our Mom Is Getting Better*
*The Survivorship Net: A Parable for the Family, Friends, and Caregivers of People with Cancer*
*What's Up with Bridget's Mom? Medikidz Explain Breast Cancer*
*What's Up with Richard? Medikidz Explain Leukemia*

Visit **cancer.org/bookstore** for a full listing
of books published by the American Cancer Society.